THE THREE BILLY
ꓯATS GRUFF

First published in Great Britain by HarperCollins Publishers Ltd in 1991
First published in this edition in Picture Lions in 1996
3 5 7 9 10 8 6 4 2
Picture Lions is an imprint of the Children's Division, part of HarperCollins
Publishers Ltd, 77-85 Fulham Palace Road, Hammersmith, London W6 8JB.
Text and illustrations copyright © Jonathan Langley 1991
The author/illustrator asserts the moral right to
be identified as the author/illustrator of the work.
ISBN: 0 00 664250 0
Printed in Italy by L.E.G.O.

THE THREE BILLY GOATS GRUFF

RETOLD & ILLUSTRATED BY
JONATHAN LANGLEY

PictureLions

An Imprint of HarperCollins*Publishers*

Once upon a time, in a land beyond the high mountains and over the sea, there were three billy goats who lived on a rocky hillside. There was a big billy goat, a middle-sized billy goat, and a little billy goat, and they were all called Gruff.

The three Billy Goats Gruff had always lived on the
hillside and every day they did nothing but eat from
morning till night. The other goats who lived there
were happy to eat the rough grass that grew between the
stones, the moss that grew on the rocks, and the leaves
and twigs that grew on the trees; but the three Billy Goats
Gruff wanted more.

They dreamed of going down into the valley, trotting
across the bridge which joined the rocky hillside to the
lush green meadow on the other side of the river and
eating until they were fat.

But the bridge was the only way across
the river, which was deep and fast flowing,
and under the bridge lived a Troll.
He was as frightening to look at as he was
fierce and would gobble up anyone
who tried to cross to the other side
and no one dared to try.

One day, when the three Billy Goats Gruff were again moaning about the coarse grass and dry leaves, an old grandfather billy goat, who was eating nearby, laughed and said,

"Perhaps you should all go and feast yourselves in the big meadow."

"Perhaps we should!" replied the little Billy Goat Gruff, cheekily.

"And what about the river?" said the grandfather billy goat. "And the Troll?"

"I'm not afraid of the Troll," said the big Billy Goat Gruff.

"Neither am I," said the middle-sized Billy Goat Gruff.

"Nor me," said the little Billy Goat Gruff. "We'll go right now!"

The other two Billy Goats Gruff looked at the little Billy Goat Gruff, then at each other. They hadn't intended this to happen and were rather shocked.

"Well, are all you brave Billy Goats Gruff going?" taunted the grandfather billy goat.

"Er... yes, of course we are," said the big Billy Goat Gruff. "We're not frightened."

Really they were all very frightened, but now they had to go, or look foolish.

"Goodbye, Billy Goats Gruff. I don't expect we'll see you again," said the old grandfather billy goat.

The three Billy Goats Gruff started off down the hillside,
slowly at first, then faster and faster as it became a race to
the bottom.

When they reached the river they looked at the deep
rushing water. If only they could swim across, they all
thought. They gazed over at the green meadow. It made
them feel hungry, but also afraid.

They looked again across the river. The sun was shining
on the lush green grass and clover and speckles of sweet
flowers sparkled in the sunlight.

Determinedly they made their way along the river bank
to the big wooden bridge.

Standing well back, they tried to look underneath at what might be lurking in the shadows, but it was too dark and gloomy to see.

(Deep within the darkness lay the Troll asleep. He'd been fishing all night but had caught nothing, which had made him very grumpy.)

"Perhaps the Troll has gone away?" said the little Billy Goat Gruff hopefully.

"Perhaps he has," said the middle-sized Billy Goat Gruff. "Since this was your idea, you go first and see. We'll just wait here."

The middle-sized Billy Goat Gruff and the big Billy Goat Gruff stepped back, leaving the little Billy Goat Gruff standing alone.

The little Billy Goat Gruff was afraid. He turned to look at his brothers, then, with his head held high, bravely set off across the bridge.

TRIP, TRAP! TRIP, TRAP! TRIP, TRAP! TRIP, TRAP! went his hooves on the wooden boards. He was nearly in the middle and thought he was going to get safely across when suddenly the monstrous Troll popped his head out from beneath the bridge.

"Who's that trip-trapping over my bridge?" roared the Troll, rubbing his eyes.

"It's only me," said the little Billy Goat Gruff in his little voice, "I'm going across to the meadow to make myself fat."

"Oh no you're not!" roared the Troll. "You've woken me up and now I'm coming to gobble you up!"

"No, no, don't eat me," bleated the little Billy Goat Gruff. "I'm the littlest Billy Goat Gruff. I'm too small and bony. Wait until the second Billy Goat Gruff comes along. He's much bigger and fatter."

"Very well," said the Troll angrily, "be off with you!"

So the little Billy Goat Gruff crossed the bridge and skipped off into the meadow to eat the sweet grass.

When the middle-sized Billy Goat Gruff saw that his brother had reached the meadow safely, he felt much braver and he too set off across the bridge.

TRIP, TRAP! TRIP, TRAP! TRIP, TRAP! TRIP, TRAP! went his hooves on the wooden boards. He was nearly in the middle when again out popped the Troll's head, looking very fierce, from beneath the bridge.

"Who's that trip-trapping over my bridge?"
roared the Troll.

"It's only me," said the middle-sized Billy Goat Gruff
in his middle-sized voice. "I'm going across to the
meadow to make myself fat."

"Oh no you're not!" roared the Troll. "I'm coming to gobble you up!"

"No, no, don't eat me," pleaded the middle-sized Billy Goat Gruff. "I'm not a very big Billy Goat Gruff. There's a much bigger one than me. Wait until the third Billy Goat Gruff comes along. He's much bigger and fatter."

"Very well," said the Troll even angrier, "be off with you!"

So the middle-sized Billy Goat Gruff crossed the bridge and skipped off into the meadow to join his brother eating the sweet grass.

Then there was only the big Billy Goat Gruff left to cross. He puffed himself up to make him feel very strong and brave, then he too set off across the bridge.

TRIP, TRAP! TRIP, TRAP! TRIP, TRAP! TRIP, TRAP! stamped his hooves on the wooden boards. He was nearly in the middle when, once again, out popped the Troll's head looking fiercer than ever.

"Who's that trip-trapping over my bridge?" roared the Troll.

"It's me, the biggest Billy Goat Gruff," bellowed the big Billy Goat Gruff in his great big voice, "and I'm going across to the meadow to make myself fat!"

"Oh no you're not!" roared the Troll, even louder than before, "I'm coming to gobble you up!"

The Troll leapt up onto the bridge and started gnashing his teeth but the big Billy Goat Gruff stamped his hooves, then lowered his horns, and charged!

Thundering over the wooden boards, with steam coming out of his nostrils, he tossed the Troll high in the air. Up, up he went, so high he circled the moon, then down, down he fell – SPLASH! – into the middle of the deep river and was never seen again.

The Big Billy Goat Gruff crossed the bridge and skipped off into the meadow to join his brothers.

Then the three Billy Goats Gruff ate the sweet grass until they were fat, and then they ate until their tummies hurt, and then they ate until they couldn't move, and then they went to sleep for a long, long time.

The three Billy Goats Gruff had a long and happy life. They all grew up to be old grandfather Billy Goats Gruff with great curling horns and long grey beards.

Sometimes they went back over the bridge to see their friends on the rocky hillside, but whenever they did, they galloped across as fast as they could just in case the Troll had come back.